W9-AAT-314

THIS TREE COUNTS!

Alison Formento   Illustrated **by Sarah Snow**

www.av2books.com

Your AV² Media Enhanced book gives you a fiction readalong online. Log on to www.av2books.com and enter the unique book code from this page to use your readalong.

AV² Readalong Navigation

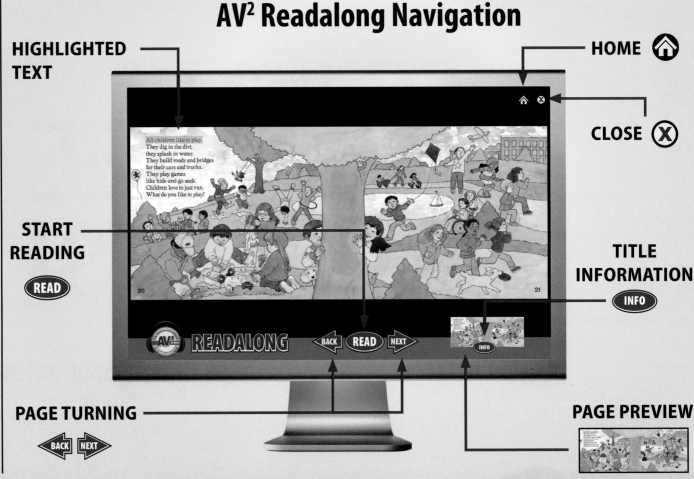

HIGHLIGHTED TEXT

HOME

CLOSE

START READING

READ

TITLE INFORMATION

INFO

PAGE TURNING

PAGE PREVIEW

Go to **www.av2books.com**, and enter this book's unique code.

BOOK CODE

N 4 1 5 2 8 1

AV² **by Weigl** brings you media enhanced books that support active learning.

First Published by

ALBERT WHITMAN & COMPANY
Publishing children's books since 1919

Published by AV² by Weigl
350 5ᵗʰ Avenue, 59ᵗʰ Floor New York, NY 10118
Website: www.av2books.com   www.weigl.com

Library of Congress Control Number: 2013940110

ISBN 978-1-62127-902-0 (hardcover)
ISBN 978-1-48961-479-7 (single-user eBook)
ISBN 978-1-48961-480-3 (multi-user eBook)

Printed in the United States of America in North Mankato, Minnesota
1 2 3 4 5 6 7 8 9 0   17 16 15 14 13

052013
WEP250413

Text copyright ©2010 by Alison Formento.
Illustrations copyright ©2010 by Sarah Snow.
Published in 2010 by Albert Whitman & Company.

Only one tree stood behind Oak Lane School.
It needed friends.

THE
OAK LANE
SCHOOL

3

So Mr. Tate's class decided to plant more trees.

The children got ready to dig.
Mr. Tate said, "Wait! Our big tree has a story to tell."

The wind began to blow, and
the giant tree shook its leaves.
"Trees can't talk," Jake said.
Mr. Tate said, "Trees will speak
only if you listen closely."

Everyone leaned an ear
against the tree. This is
what they heard...

5

One owl sits high on my branches,
waiting for the moon.

6

Two spiders cling tight to webs, spinning all day long.

7

Three squirrels skitter across my boughs,
playing hide-and-seek.

8

Four robins sing from a nest, calling out hellos.

Five caterpillars inch by, building new cocoons.

"They'll turn into butterflies soon," Shin said.
"Shhh!" said Eli. "The tree wants us to listen."

Six ants march from leaf to leaf, crawling along my bark.

12

Seven *crickets rub strong long legs, chirping at the sun.*

Eight *flies buzz all around, searching for some food.*

13

Nine ladybugs climb around my trunk, exploring before they fly.

14

Ten earthworms glide over my roots, munching rich moist soil.

I am a home for so many, all living safe and free!

Everyone looked up at the giant tree.
It waved its leaves.

One fell on Amy's head.

16

"What did you hear?" Mr. Tate asked.
"This tree counts!" Jake said.

"What else is great about trees?" Mr. Tate asked.
"They make cool shade," said Natalie.
"This tree washes the air, too," said Mr. Tate.
"Trees can't wash," Jake said.

"They do wash!" Mr. Tate said. "They take in
dirty air and send out fresh oxygen to breathe."

Everyone took a deep breath.

"This tree is so pretty. Can we name it?" Natalie asked.
"Trees don't have names," Jake said.
"They do have names!" said Mr. Tate. "We call this an oak.
That's what we're planting today. These oak saplings will grow and make acorns."

"Squirrels love acorns," Jake said. "They gather them in the fall."
"That's right," Mr. Tate said. "And the ones they don't eat, you can plant to grow your own oak trees. Can you think of some other kinds of trees?"

20

"We have an apple tree in our yard," Shin said.

"Palm trees grow where it's warm," said Eli.

"What about Christmas trees?" Jake asked.
"Those are fir trees," Mr. Tate said.
"They stay green all year long."

"This tree is so big," Natalie said. "I wish I could live up there."
"I have a tree house," Eli said. "I made up a poem about it."

Tree house, tree house, in the sky,
grow some wings and you can fly!
Birds can nest, and so can I.

Jake put his arms around the tree. He looked up through the branches. "Trees sure can do a lot!"

Mr. Tate nodded. "Now you're ready to dig."

Everyone planted…

one, two, three,
four, five, six,
seven, eight, nine,
ten trees.

Ten baby trees.

"Have fun with your new friends," Shin told the giant tree.
The wind blew, and the tree waved again.

The new trees waved, too!